For Noah and Eleanor

In memory of
Susan, Bruce, Carol and Troy

If I Had a Giant Toe...

BY Jill D. Clark

Illustrated by Lynda Farrington Wilson

If I had a giant toe
gigantic as can be
imagine all the things I'd do.
The possibility!

I'd zoom along at lightning pace.
I'd beat a cheetah in a race.

I'd outrun all the kids at school,
outswim a dolphin in a pool...

...swing like a monkey in a zoo,
jump higher than a kangaroo!

I'd be a giant superstar,
travel the world
both near and far...

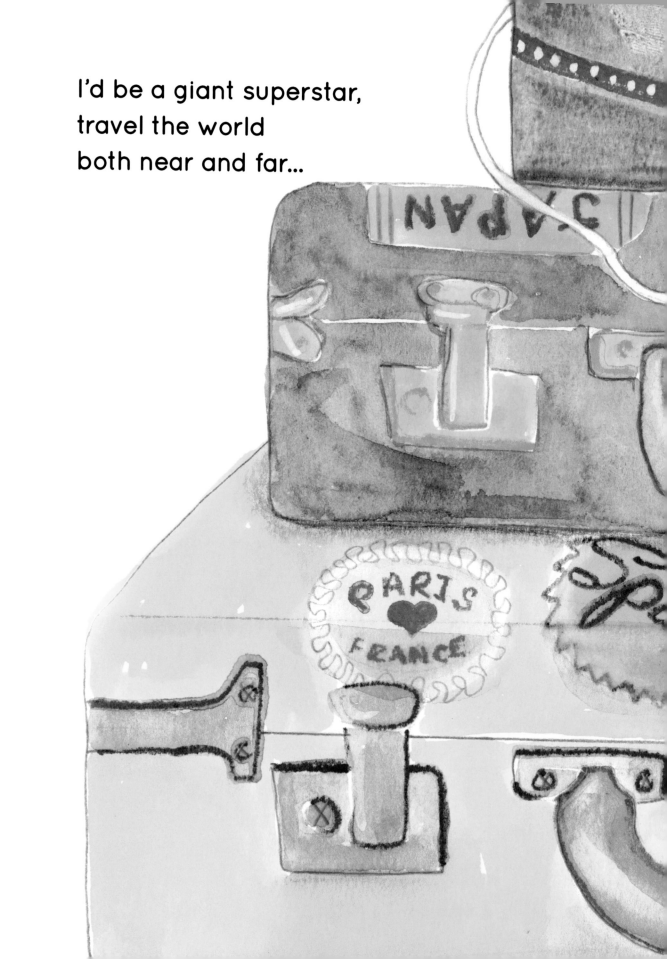

...or join the circus as a clown.
I'd be the biggest talk of town!

It's clear I have
this figured out.
There's not one little
shred of doubt
that everyone
would want to be
giant-toed just like me!

But if I had a giant toe,
would socks and shoes still fit?

Oh no!

Or would I have
two strange
left feet
when dancing to
a rhythmic beat?

What would I call
my giant toe?
Pinky, or Moe
or Curly Joe?

To market would that piggy go?
Or stay at home and just lay low?

Would that toe eat roast beef or not?
Oh gee my brain is in a knot!

In the end, I'm glad I'm me,
the way that I was made to be.

But we are all unique, you see,
from giant toes to ten or three,
eleven, eight, or five or none—
We're perfect! Each and every one!

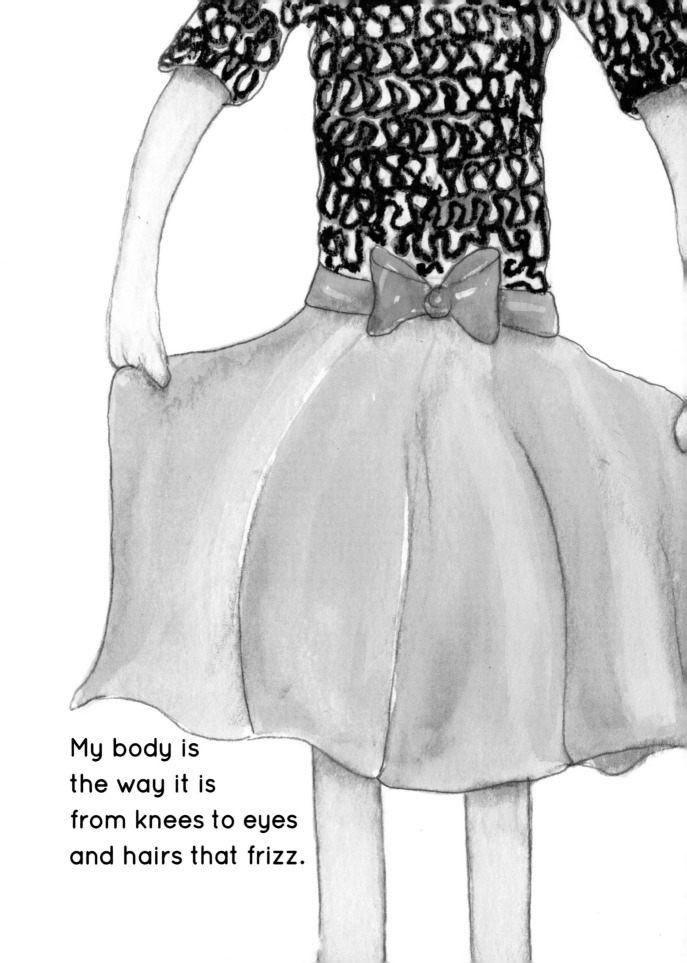

My body is
the way it is
from knees to eyes
and hairs that frizz.

But one
more thing
I've asked
for years.

What if I had...

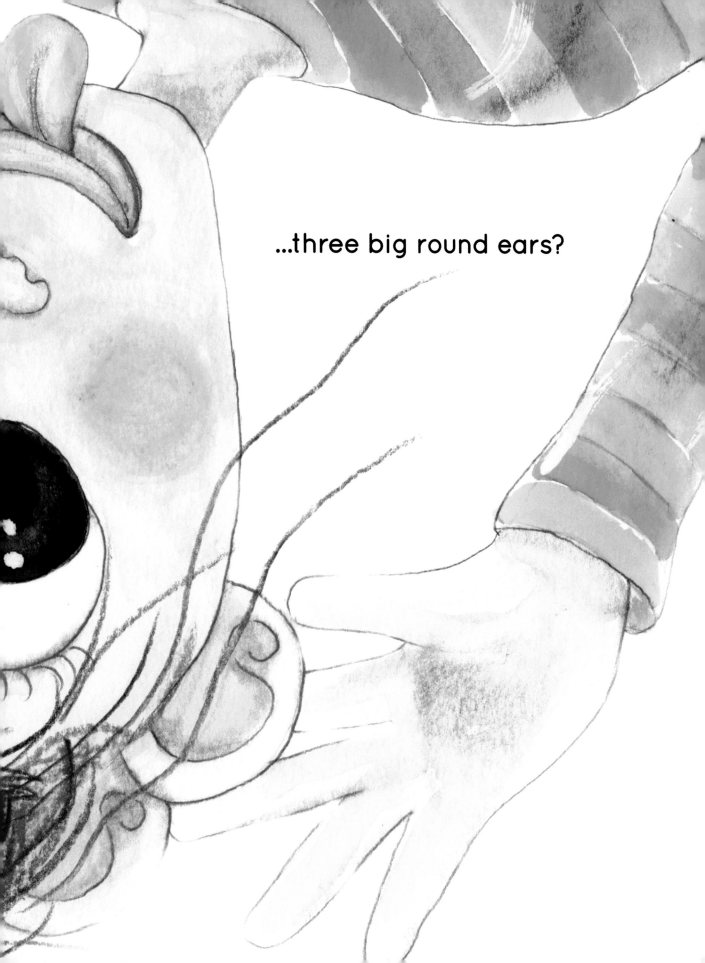

...three big round ears?

About The Author

Jill Clark is a God-fearing, out-door-loving, Netflix-binging, friend and family-obsessed parent of twins, Noah and Eleanor. She is married to her fabulous husband, Brent, and together they live in St. Louis, Missouri, with said goofball twins.

Jill has been writing professionally for nearly 10 years, specifically in the world of education. Her writing has appeared in chapter books, edited volumes, journals, magazines and blogs.

If I Had A Giant Toe is Jill's first venture into children's writing.

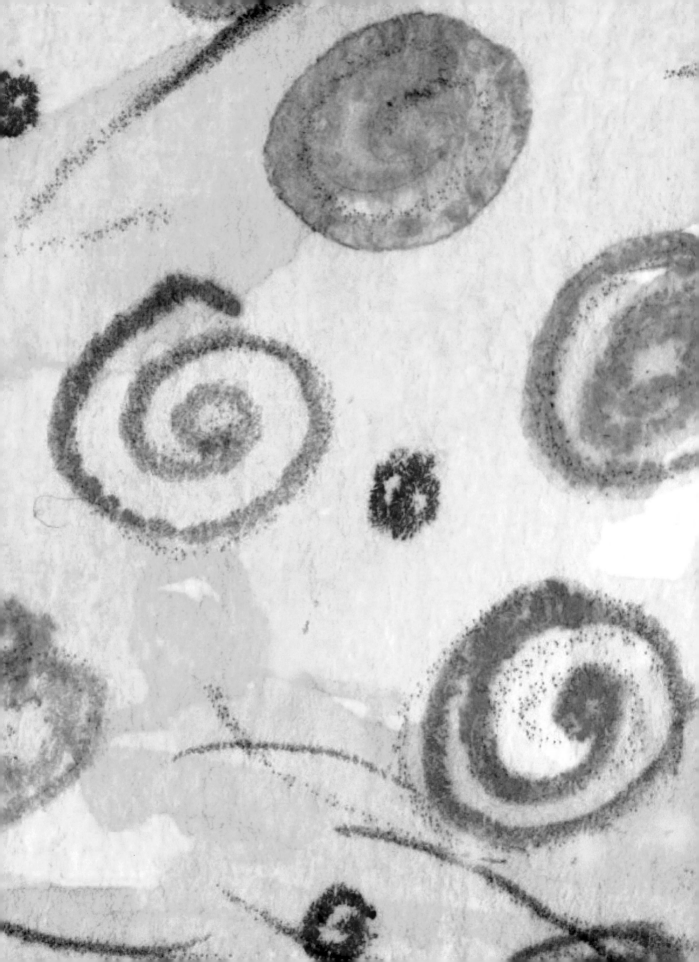

Made in the USA
Columbia, SC
24 October 2018